D1065051

*P*ainfully shy **Beth March** is excited to be visiting New York City with her parents. The theater, opera, symphony, museums—Beth loves every minute of her adventure. She even meets Abraham Lincoln, and has the courage to tell him that women deserve the right to vote. But once she's back home in Massachusetts, none of Beth's schoolmates believe that she really spoke to Mr. Lincoln, or that she even met him. They know Beth is shy— too shy to talk to a man running for president of the United States. Even Beth's younger sister, Amy, thinks she's lying. Now Beth wishes she'd never been to New York . . . until she's surprised by an unexpected visitor.

PORTRAITS
of LITTLE WOMEN
Beth's Story

Don't miss any of the
Portraits of Little Women

Meg's Story

Jo's Story

Beth's Story

Amy's Story

PORTRAITS
of LITTLE WOMEN
Beth's Story

Susan Beth Pfeffer

DELACORTE PRESS

Published by
Delacorte Press
Bantam Doubleday Dell Publishing Group, Inc.
1540 Broadway
New York, New York 10036

Library of Congress Cataloging-in-Publication Data

Pfeffer, Susan Beth.
Portraits of Little Women, Beth's story/Susan Beth Pfeffer.
p.   cm.
Based on characters found in Louisa May Alcott's Little Women.
Summary: Relates ten-year-old Beth's exciting trip to pre–Civil War
New York City with Marmee and Father.
ISBN 0-385-32526-6
[1. Sisters—Fiction.   2. Family life—Fiction.   3. New York (N.Y.)—
Description and travel—Fiction.]   4. New York (N.Y.)—History—1775–
1865—Fiction.]   I. Alcott, Louisa May, 1832–1888. Little Women.
II. Title.
PZ7.P44855Pl   1997
[Fic]—dc21   97-6146
                                                                      CIP
                                                                       AC

The text of this book is set in 13-point Cochin.

Cover and text design by Patrice Sheridan
Cover illustration copyright © 1997 by Lori Earley
Text illustrations copyright © 1997 by Marcy Ramsey
Activities illustrations copyright © 1997 by Laura Maestro

Manufactured in the United States of America

November 1997

10   9   8   7   6   5   4   3   2   1

BVG

FOR RUTH FREHNER

PORTRAITS
of LITTLE WOMEN
Beth's Story

CHAPTER 1

"*I* do believe," Father March said, looking at his wife and their four daughters as they finished eating their supper, "that this is my favorite part of the day."

"Mine too," his second-oldest daughter, Jo, said. "It means school is over and so are our tasks, and we can spend the evening however we want."

"I like the mornings best," said Amy, the youngest of the girls. "The light is better then for drawing. Of course, in February there's hardly any light at any time of day. I like mornings best in the summer."

"I like midafternoon the best," Meg, the oldest, said. "Even on a cold winter's day. It's the warmest time of the day, and the sun shines the brightest."

"What about you, Bethy?" Marmee asked. "What is your favorite time of day?"

"I don't have a favorite," Beth replied. "It would be like having a favorite sister. Each is wonderful in her own way. So is each time of day."

Marmee laughed. "I agree with Beth," she said. "Morning, noon, and night—they each have something to recommend them."

"And like your daughters, they each could stand a little improvement!" Jo said, and they all joined in her laughter.

"Nonetheless," Father said, "to sit here after one of Hannah's fine suppers, and to look at my wife and my four beautiful daughters—this is contentment of the purest kind."

"Notice how he puts supper first," Jo said. "Wife and daughters come after a full stomach."

"But the joy I get from my wife and daughters is a constant," replied her father. "And supper comes but once a day."

"He has you there, Jo," Meg said.

"But I fear this contentment will not last forever," said Father.

"Why not?" asked Beth, who was always fearful of change.

"He means we'll grow up," Meg said, "and marry and have families of our own." That was her dream.

"Not for a while, I should think," said Jo. "You're thirteen, Meg, and I'm twelve. I don't think Father approves of child brides."

"He said it wouldn't last forever," said Meg, "not that it was about to end next week."

"But next week is just when it will end," said Father.

His four daughters fell silent. Beth felt fear clutch her. Was Father going to leave? Where would he be going?

"Your father is teasing you," Marmee said. She reached out to give Beth's hand a reassuring pat. "We're going to take a trip, that's all."

"A trip?" Jo asked. "Where to? Are we all to come along?"

"Your mother and I are going to New York City," replied Father. "We'll take the train there next week and stay for a week."

"How exciting!" Meg exclaimed. "Will you shop while you're there? Marmee, I hear the stores in New York are almost equal to those in London and Paris."

"And they're every bit as expensive," said Marmee. "I'll look around for bargains, but I doubt I'll find any. However, that's not the reason for the trip."

"What is, then?" asked Amy.

"There are several reasons, actually," Father said. "As you girls know, there is fear of a possible war in this country. The Southern states want to continue the expansion of slavery, and of course many of us in the North want slavery abolished altogether. Several of my friends here have asked me to go to New

York to speak with some of the leading abolitionists, Mr. Horace Greeley and the Reverend Henry Beecher, for example, to determine what they think is likely to happen and to find out what we and they can do in the event of a war to see to it that slavery is finally ended."

"Mr. Greeley and Mr. Beecher!" Meg said. "They're both so famous. Do you know them, Father?"

"I've met them both, yes," Father said. "And we've exchanged letters recently. They agree it's a good idea for us to speak. This is an election year, and there are those who believe that if Mr. Lincoln is elected president, civil war will follow."

"And a jolly good thing it would be," said Jo. "I only wish I were a boy so I could fight for the rights of the slaves."

"War is never a jolly good thing, Jo," her father declared, "no matter how just the cause. I pray that a peaceable solution will be found, but I fear none will be."

"So you'll be speaking to Mr. Greeley, and

Marmee will be looking for bargains," Meg said. "It still sounds like a wonderful trip."

"It's more wonderful than that," Marmee said. "We'll be staying with my friend Mrs. Webster. Her daughter, Catherine, is engaged to marry a gentleman named Mr. Kirke."

"Are you going for the wedding?" asked Meg.

"I'm going to help prepare the trousseau," Marmee replied. "And to visit with my old friend. Mrs. Webster owns a boardinghouse, so there will be plenty of room for us to stay."

"And you'll be gone for a whole week, Marmee?" Beth asked. She knew she should be happy for her parents to have such an exciting trip planned, but she already missed them.

"A week," said Father. "Hardly enough time for all that's planned."

"What else will you be doing?" asked Amy.

"We want to go to the theater," Marmee said. "Edwin Booth is playing in *Hamlet*. And Mrs. Webster says we simply must see a production of *Uncle Tom's Cabin*. You know, the novel was written by Mr. Beecher's sister, Harriet Stowe. And what I think is most exciting of all, your father has agreed to have his photograph taken."

"Really?" Jo said.

"Mr. Emerson thinks it's a good idea," her father replied.

"And so do I," said Marmee. "I know I'll cherish a photograph of my handsome husband. And Mathew Brady, the most important photographer in this country, has consented to take the picture."

"What a week," said Meg. "The theater, politics, a trousseau, Mathew Brady, and shopping!"

"I never thought Meg would put shopping last on her list of pleasures," Jo said, and they all laughed, even Meg.

"But there's one other thing to make it more perfect," said Father. "Your mother and I have gone over the expenses for the trip several times, and we agree that if we're careful about how we spend our money, we can afford to take one of you along."

"A week in New York!" cried Jo. "Oh, take me, please."

"No, me," said Amy.

"I should love it also," Meg said. "And I love to sew. I could help with the trousseau."

Beth only smiled.

"We suspected you would all want to go," said Marmee. "So we've decided to let you girls choose who will get to spend a week in New York with us."

Beth looked at her sisters, all brimming with excitement. It would be a hard choice, but she knew whoever was selected would be the most deserving of the treat.

CHAPTER 2

*M*eg, Jo, Beth, and Amy gathered in Meg and Jo's bedroom after dinner. Usually the family sang songs together while Beth played the piano, but this evening the four sisters were too excited and begged to be allowed to go and decide which of them would be the lucky one to accompany their parents.

"Choose wisely," Marmee had said, giving each of her daughters a good-night kiss. "And remember that New York will still be there, and each of you will have a chance to go at some time in your life."

"Yes, Marmee," they had all said, but Beth knew each of her sisters wanted to go to New York next week and not have to wait for some hard-to-imagine long time away.

"Obviously I should go," Meg said, before any of them had the chance to speak. She and Amy had curled up in Meg's bed to keep warm on the cold winter's night. "I'd be the most help to Marmee with the trousseau. Besides, I'm the oldest, so I deserve it most."

"Hogwash," said Jo.

"Jo, please, no slang," said Meg.

But Jo ignored her, as she always did. She and Beth were sharing Jo's bed, and Jo was so irate at Meg's argument that she sat upright and pulled the blankets away from Beth. "Hogwash, hogwash, hogwash," Jo said. "I know how to sew also, Meg. And I'm much more interested in politics than you. I need to go more than you do, to see all those plays. How can you expect me to be a great writer if all I ever see of life is Concord, Massachusetts? And the very fact that you're the oldest means you shouldn't go. You'll have your chance so much sooner than the rest of us because of your age. I wager you and your husband will take your wedding trip to New York just so that you can shop there. Which is another good reason you shouldn't go and I should. You'll make Marmee shop all day long and she'll never get anything done and she'll spend far more money than she should. That always happens when you and Marmee shop together in Boston. No, I should go. I'm sure that's obvious to all of us."

"It isn't obvious to me," said Amy. "What's obvious to me is that I should go."

"Why am I not surprised?" Jo muttered.

"First of all, I agree with Jo about Meg's not going because she is the oldest," Amy said. "She'll have her chance far sooner than any of the rest of us. And I'm the youngest and I never get to do anything for just that reason. So I should be the one to go. And what Jo said about needing to travel is even truer of an artist. Whoever heard of a great painter staying in Concord? I simply have to travel if my art is to be great. I may not sew as well as Meg or be as interested in politics as Jo, but I could make lovely sketches of Mrs. Webster and Catherine. I won't force Marmee to look for endless bargains. Nor will I say foolish things about how jolly war is. I'm the perfect choice to go."

Meg looked over at Beth. "What do you think?" Meg asked.

"I think all of you are right," Beth said, marveling that each of her sisters had such good reasons for going, while all Beth wanted was a chance to go to a concert. "I wish you could all go, though I'd be miserable if you did and I was left alone."

Jo laughed. "Why don't we vote?" she said. "Then we can see where we stand. How many think Meg should go?"

Meg alone raised her hand.

"And Amy?" Jo asked.

Amy's hand went up.

"Well, I vote for me to go," said Jo. "Bethy, will you vote for me?"

Beth loved all her sisters dearly, but she had a special spot in her heart for Jo. Still, it seemed unfair that Jo should be allowed to go and Meg and Amy, both of whose arguments had been quite convincing, should be made to stay at home.

"No," Beth said. "I'm sorry, Jo. I can't be the one to decide which one of you goes."

"We could draw lots," Amy said.

"That would be gambling," Meg said. "I think Father and Marmee would prefer it if we could decide by talking it out."

"We can talk it to death," Amy said, "and we'll each still vote for ourselves."

"No," Jo said, looking first at Amy, then at Meg, then at Beth. "I think there's an obvious answer to our problem. I'll change my vote."

"Oh, Jo!" Meg said. "I'll never forget this. And when I'm in New York, I'll be sure to pay attention to every single thing and tell you about it, so that you can use it in your writing."

"Don't be so sure I'm going to vote for you," said Jo.

"Thank you, Jo!" Amy cried. "I'll do better than Meg. I'll sketch everything I see, and you can use my pictures when you write about New York!"

"I might not be voting for you either," said Jo.

"Then who?" Meg asked.

"I'm voting for Beth," Jo declared. "I think she should go to New York with Father and Marmee."

"Beth?" Amy said. "She doesn't even want to go."

"She never said she didn't want to," Jo said. "And it's just like Beth to put our happiness ahead of hers. You see it, don't you, Meg? If you go, Amy and I will resent it. And if I go, you and Amy will resent it. And if Amy goes, you and I will resent it. But if Beth goes, we'll all be a little bit jealous, but mostly we'll be happy for her."

"Jo's right," Meg said. "Beth is always doing kind things for others and never asking anything for herself. I vote for Beth to go."

"Beth," Amy said, "you don't have to vote for yourself, you know. You can vote for me."

"Don't be a selfish beast," Jo said. "Beth, whom do you vote for?"

"I can't vote for myself," Beth said. "It doesn't seem right. But I can't pick among you either. So I still won't vote."

"Very well," Jo said. "Meg and I vote for Beth. Amy, are you still voting for yourself?"

"Does it matter?" Amy asked. "I'm bound to lose."

"I think Marmee and Father would be pleased if we could tell them we were unanimous about Beth's going," Meg said. "Do you think you could do that for them?"

Amy sighed. "Someday I'll be a great artist," she said. "And a fabulously rich lady. No thanks to any of you. All right. I vote for Beth to go to New York. I suppose it's better than Jo, at least."

"Hurrah!" cried Jo. "Our Bethy is going to New York. And we hardly came close to a civil war to decide it."

Beth hugged Jo and then Meg, who had hopped out of her bed to show her affection for her younger sister. Amy scowled and left for the bedroom she and Beth shared.

"She'll get over it," Jo said. "Amy really isn't selfish. She'll be happy for you soon enough."

Beth hoped so. No trip to New York was worth the loss of her little sister's love.

CHAPTER 3

"Good-bye, Hannah," Beth said to their housekeeper, trying to hold back the tears that filled her eyes.

Hannah squeezed her tightly. "You enjoy yourself in New York," she said. "And see to it your parents do more than work."

"I will," Beth promised. She thought her heart would break at the thought of being away from home for a whole week.

Meg and Jo seemed to feel the same way about missing Beth. They embraced her as though she were going off to war. Only Amy held back, which made Beth feel even sadder.

"I wish it were you going," she whispered to Amy.

"I wish it were too," Amy said, giving Beth a cold kiss on her cheek.

It took a while before the farewells were completed. Marmee had a thousand last-minute instructions for her daughters as well as for Hannah. Finally Father and Mr. Emerson, who was taking them to the train station in his carriage, began to look impatient.

Marmee wiped a tear from her eye as the carriage bore them away from their home. "I know I'm being foolish," she said, "but a week seems like such a long time to me now."

"It will go by in a flash," Mr. Emerson said.

Beth felt better hearing that. She loved and trusted Mr. Emerson, her father's best friend, and if he was so sure time would pass rapidly, then he was undoubtedly right.

Besides, it was a great adventure, and although Beth had never thought of herself as the adventurous type, it was still exciting to go to New York City, the biggest city in the

United States. She comforted herself by imagining her return and how she would bring her sisters mementos from New York. And despite her shyness, she was very interested in going to the theater and meeting the Reverend Henry Beecher.

They took the train to Boston, which Beth had done a few times before, and then took a far grander train from Boston to New York. She and her parents shared their section with a family of six.

Beth watched as the other children fought with each other over every little thing. One of the older boys even hit his baby sister with her doll.

Beth huddled closer to Marmee. She was glad she had resisted temptation and left all her dolls at home. She'd come close to packing Annabelle, her current favorite, but Amy had given her a scathing look when she'd picked Annabelle up to place her in her valise, and Beth had quickly put Annabelle back with her other dolls.

Now she was relieved that she had. Who knew what a boy like that would do with Annabelle? And since Annabelle was already missing a leg, Beth was sure the doll would not have survived any activity on the part of their section mates.

Marmee and Hannah had packed a lunch for them, so when the train made its stops, they chose not to purchase food, although they did get out to use the facilities and stretch their legs.

"The food is so dreadfully overpriced," Marmee said. "It makes me worry about how much this trip is going to cost."

"We have it all budgeted," Father said. "So long as we economize on big expenditures, we'll be able to afford the little luxuries."

"Like food!" Marmee exclaimed merrily.

"I meant the theater," said Father, but he laughed at the thought of food's being a luxury.

Beth tried to remember if she'd ever seen her parents quite so jolly before. She didn't think so. But then she could hardly remember a time when she had been alone with them. There was always one sister or another around, and even if there wasn't, Father's work as a minister and Marmee's charity work kept the house full of visitors.

Beth looked at all the people who had gotten off the train. The more elegant people had gone to the first-class dining room, but Beth was positive that no matter how finely dressed those people might be, her parents were the best-looking people there. She knew vanity was a sin and that it didn't matter how you looked—what mattered was whether you were good—but she didn't care. She was delighted with her handsome parents—parents who were very much in love.

The train trip took many hours, but Beth and the other children napped during the long afternoon. When she awoke, she was annoyed at herself for missing so much of the journey, especially since she had a seat by a window and had been enjoying seeing the countryside rush by. She felt better when Marmee confessed that she too had fallen asleep.

"I hope you don't intend to sleep this trip away," said Father with an affectionate smile.

"On the contrary," Marmee said. "I've refreshed myself so that I can stay up to the wee hours of the morning, while you will be exhausted and in need of twelve hours' sleep each night."

"We'll see which one of us is more exhausted in the morning!" said Father, and, ignoring the presence of all the others in their compartment, gave his wife a big kiss.

Marmee blushed bright red, but Beth had never felt happier in her life.

"Now, stay by my side," Father said as the train reached the station in New York. "We don't want to lose each other."

"Certainly not," said Marmee. "Beth, hold my hand. Father, can you manage all our luggage by yourself?"

"I believe so," he said. "What a madhouse this is."

Beth agreed. There were hundreds of people milling about the station. Porters were helping to carry the trunks of many of the passengers, but Father declined their assistance.

"Look at that child," Marmee said, gesturing to a boy who was selling matches. "He looks younger than Amy."

Father walked over to the boy. Beth couldn't hear what he said, the noise at the station was so great, but when he returned to her and Marmee he was carrying quite a few boxes of matches.

"Dearest, did you leave us any money at all?" Marmee asked.

Father smiled. "I'm afraid we'll have to take the horsecar and not a hackney cab to the Webster' house," he admitted. "It seemed like a small sacrifice to make when that lad probably has no home to call his own."

"You're right," Marmee said. "But if you sacrifice too much, then food will indeed be a luxury on this trip."

"I promise to be a regular miser from now

on," Father said. "You and Beth will want for nothing for the remainder of the week."

"It doesn't matter to me," Beth said, and she meant it. She could walk to the Websters' and be just as glad. She was in New York City for the greatest adventure of her life.

CHAPTER 4

*M*armee and Mrs. Webster exchanged warm embraces upon the March family's arrival at Mrs. Webster's home. "I've put you in two rooms on the third floor," Mrs. Webster said. "I hope you don't mind being so high up, but I couldn't displace any of my regular customers."

"The third floor is fine," said Father, who carried the bags upstairs, refusing the help of one of the maids. Beth followed him. There was a large bedroom for her parents and a small sitting room, where a bed had been placed, for Beth. Beth couldn't remember ever having a room to herself, and she was glad her parents were just a door away.

Beth, Father, and Marmee refreshed themselves, then joined Mrs. Webster and her daughter, Catherine, in the parlor. "This is so kind of you," Catherine said. "Mother and I have been working on the trousseau every chance we get, but the boardinghouse keeps us both so busy that we start one piece and never seem to get it finished."

"And the wedding is in less than a month," Mrs. Webster said. "But please don't spend all your time in the house with us. There are so many sights to see in New York."

"And tomorrow we'll see as many of them as we can," Father said. "Then on Sunday we'll go to the Reverend Beecher's church in Brooklyn."

"You'll need to take the steam ferry to get there," said Catherine. "Have you ever been on a ferry, Beth?"

Beth shook her head. She was always shy with strangers, and though the Websters looked like the friendliest of people, it was hard for her to actually speak to them.

"It will be just one more adventure for us," said Marmee. "But starting Monday, I'll work on the trousseau. Mr. March has his appointment with Mathew Brady that day, and the day following that with Mr. Greeley."

"Such important men," said Catherine. "I've lived in New York all my life and never met anyone half so grand."

"Except for Mr. Kirke," her mother said.

Catherine blushed prettily. "Except for Mr. Kirke," she agreed.

Mrs. Webster had prepared a light supper for them, and after eating it Beth was ready to go to bed. She lingered a little, enjoying the sight and sound of her parents in such a relaxed setting, but then she made her way to her room, and in spite of the strange environment and her being all alone, she fell sound asleep moments after her head had touched the pillow.

✳   ✳   ✳

"Now you go off and have a wonderful day," Mrs. Webster said the next morning as Beth and her parents prepared to set out on their adventure. "I'll see you tonight, and I expect to hear every single detail."

"Late tonight," Father said. "We'll be going to the theater."

"I won't wait up for you, then," said Mrs. Webster. "Save your stories for Sunday dinner."

It was a cold February day, but there was no wind, and the sun was shining down as strongly as it could manage.

"Let's stroll down Broadway and look at the sights," Father suggested.

"That sounds wonderful," Marmee said. "Of course, right now, everything sounds wonderful."

Beth walked between her parents. She couldn't get over the vastness of everything. There were buildings six stories high! Her neck began to hurt from the strain of looking up at every one of them. Her feet also hurt from walking on the cobblestoned streets. But she didn't care. There were so many things to see.

And so many people! Beth had been to Boston, so she knew what a city could be like, but New York seemed to be nothing but people. "How many people live here?" she asked her father.

"About a million, I believe," he replied. "Some rich, many poor."

"New York has even more Irish immigrants than Boston," Marmee said.

"Two hundred thousand," said Father.

"Two hundred thousand Irish," said Beth. "A million people." The numbers were so huge she couldn't begin to imagine them. "What do they all do?"

"Most of them are honest laborers," Father replied, "struggling to get by on low wages."

"Oh," Marmee said. "That reminds me. I do hope to see a sewing machine while I'm in New York. Catherine said the mother of a friend of hers has one, and it's the most re-markable invention. Can you imagine a machine that does the sewing for you?"

"Someday I'll buy you such a machine," promised Father.

"I'm not even sure I want one," said Marmee. "I love the time I spend sewing with my daughters. But I do want to see what such a marvel looks like."

"Look!" Beth said. "Isn't that Mathew Brady's studio?"

"You do have a good eye, Bethy," Father said. "It is indeed. I knew it was on Broadway. Now it will be easy for me to locate on Monday."

"And this is St. Paul's Chapel," Marmee said. "George Washington prayed here once. I wonder what he would say about our current times."

"I wonder too," Father said. "George Washington owned slaves. So many of the great men who founded this country did. If only they hadn't, there would be much less misery in this land."

"Father, what's that?" Beth asked, pointing at a building across the street.

"That's Barnum's American Museum," Marmee said. "Catherine was telling us about it last night. She and Mr. Kirke went there once. There are all sorts of freaks there, and some strange creature called the What-is-it. It seems to be something more than a chimpanzee and less than a human."

"Monday, if you like, you might go to see it," said Father, "while I sit for Mr. Brady."

"Does it cost money?" Beth asked.

"I imagine so," said Father. "But we can afford it."

"I don't think I will, then," Beth said. "I'd rather spend the money on gifts for Meg and Jo and Amy."

"That's a generous thought," Father said. "But not a surprising one, coming from you. Perhaps if our money holds out, on Thursday we can all see what Mr. Barnum has to show us."

"That would be fun," Beth agreed, relieved at the thought of not having to confront a What-is-it all by herself.

CHAPTER 5

*T*he Marches spent much of Saturday walking around, taking in the sights of New York. In the evening they went to the theater and saw Edwin Booth, the greatest actor of his time, playing Hamlet.

Beth couldn't get over the grandeur of the theater. Although she and her parents were in the highest row, it didn't seem to matter. Booth projected his voice and acted so brilliantly that Beth felt she was in Elsinore with him, trying to avenge the death of his father.

"Jo would love this," she said at intermission, as she and Marmee watched hundreds of elegantly dressed people stroll through the lobby of the theater.

"She'll have her day in New York," Marmee said. "Jo will see the world if she sets her mind to it."

Beth knew that was true, and it allowed her to enjoy the play even more. When she finally got home that night, she had trouble falling asleep, she was so tired and excited.

The next morning was a bit of a disappointment. It was snowing, and Father decided they should cancel their trip to Brooklyn and walk over to a local church instead.

"I'll meet with Mr. Beecher later this week," he said.

After services, there was a big Sunday dinner, to which all the guests of the boardinghouse were invited. Catherine's Mr. Kirke was in attendance as well, and Beth thought him a charming man, almost worthy of the warm and loving Catherine.

Between the snow and the Sabbath, the

Marches were forced to spend a quiet after-noon. So the next morning, when Beth awoke and saw that the snow had stopped, she was full of energy and the desire to see more.

"Might I go with you to Mr. Brady's studio?" she asked.

"Certainly," Father said. "If your mother approves."

"It would make me happy if you did," said Marmee. "Ask Catherine if she would care to join you, and then her mother and I would have some private time together."

Catherine was delighted to be asked along, and after breakfast she, Beth, and Father walked through the snowy streets to Mr. Brady's studio. Beth didn't know what to expect and was dazzled at the sight of a long gallery filled from floor to ceiling with photographs of famous leaders on all its walls.

The three of them looked at many of the

pictures. "Photography is a marvel of this age," Father said. "To see what all these people actually look like is thrilling. But it's also a little bit frightening."

"Why is that, Father?" Beth asked.

"Because soon I'll have to confront what I look like!" Father said. "I think I might be happier with one of Amy's sketches of me."

"It will be a handsome picture," Beth said. "As handsome as any on these walls."

Mr. March smiled. "That I doubt," he said. "But I suppose I must make peace with the nineteenth century. There are only forty years of it left."

"Just think, Beth," Catherine said. "We'll live to see the twentieth century. Imagine its marvels."

"I think I've seen enough marvels in the past two days to last me," Beth said. "And we still have the sewing machine to look forward to."

They were still laughing when a young man walked over to them and told Mr. March that Mr. Brady was ready for him.

Beth and Catherine looked at a few more pictures, then sat down on a long bench in the middle of the gallery. All the other benches were occupied.

"Do you think the other people here are famous?" Beth asked. "Should I know who they all are?"

"I know who that man is," Catherine whispered. "That tall man. He's Mr. Lincoln."

The tallest man Beth had ever seen was standing just a few feet from them. At the sound of his name, he turned to face them. "Do you young ladies mind if I join you?" he asked. "There are no other seats available."

"Please do," Catherine said. Beth could see that she was flustered.

"I believe you have the advantage over me," the man said. "I heard you call my name, but I'm afraid I don't know yours."

"Catherine Webster," Catherine said. "And this is Beth March."

"Are you really the Mr. Lincoln who wants to be president?" Beth asked. Usually Beth would be far too shy to converse with a stranger, but she was with Catherine, and Mr. Lincoln had such a kind face.

"The same," the man said.

"What brings you here from Illinois?" Catherine asked.

"I'm in New York to give a political speech," Mr. Lincoln replied. "It was scheduled for Brooklyn, at Mr. Beecher's church, but they think the crowd will be so big, they've moved it to Cooper Union, here in Manhattan."

"My father knows Mr. Beecher," Beth said. "We were going to services at his church yesterday, but the snow kept us from going."

"It's snowing again," Mr. Lincoln said. "I hope that doesn't keep the crowd away tonight."

"Is it an important speech?" Catherine asked.

Mr. Lincoln nodded. "I need to show you folks from New York that I'm not just some small-town lawyer."

"I'm not from New York," Beth said shyly. "I'm from Concord, Massachusetts. This is my very first trip here."

"It's quite a city, isn't it?" Mr. Lincoln said. "Have you been enjoying yourself?"

"I've been having the most wonderful time," Beth said. "I'm here with my parents. We're staying with Catherine at her mother's boardinghouse."

"So Miss Webster is the New Yorker," said Mr. Lincoln.

"Yes, I am," Catherine said. "And New Yorkers know you are far more than a small-town lawyer."

"I hope the other New Yorkers I meet agree with you," Mr. Lincoln said. "If I can convince them, then perhaps I'll be able to convince the rest of the nation."

"I think it must be frightening to be president now," said Catherine. "There are so many problems to be solved."

"Which issues most concern you?" Mr. Lincoln asked.

"Slavery, in particular," Catherine said. "It simply must be abolished."

"I agree with you," Mr. Lincoln said. "It is a terrible institution, one doing great harm to America."

Beth thought it was wonderful the way Catherine was telling such a famous man about the important issues of the day. It was the sort of thing Jo would do.

And she realized how disappointed Jo would be if she learned that Beth had had the chance to discuss issues with Mr. Lincoln and had been too shy to speak.

"Women should be allowed to vote," Beth said, just the way she knew Jo would. "Don't you agree, Mr. Lincoln?"

"That's a hard question," said Mr. Lincoln.

"But I promise you I'll give it a great deal of thought."

"We voted at home," Beth said. "Meg and Jo and Amy and I, to decide which one of us should go to New York. Meg and Jo both voted for me to go." She was silent for a moment, then decided against telling Mr. Lincoln that Amy had voted for herself.

"Democracy in action," Mr. Lincoln said with a smile.

"If my mother and I could vote, we would vote for you," Catherine said. "Beth's mother would too, I'm sure."

Mr. Lincoln smiled at them. "I need all the votes I can get," he said. "So I'll be certain to think about women's suffrage."

Before Beth had a chance to tell Mr. Lincoln what else he should work for, a young man came out and announced that Mr. Brady was ready for him. Beth and Catherine said good-bye to him, then waited patiently for Beth's father to come out.

"I hope you didn't mind waiting," Father said as he gathered his coat and belongings.

"Not at all," Beth said. "You can meet such interesting people in New York." And she and Catherine smiled.

CHAPTER 6

*M*r. Emerson had been right. The week went by in a flash. Father was out most of the days, paying calls on the important abolitionists, while Beth and Marmee sewed with Mrs. Webster and Catherine. The women chatted as they worked, talking about family and friends, and also about important issues.

Beth enjoyed listening to them and watching as the trousseau took form. By the end of the week all the lovely clothes were ready to be worn.

But it wasn't all work for any of the

Marches. Most evenings they went to a theater. They saw a thrilling production of *Uncle Tom's Cabin*, as well as *Rip Van Winkle* and William Burton's version of *Oliver Twist*. One night they went to the opera, and another to a concert.

And Friday afternoon, they went to Barnum's American Museum. None of the Marches was sure what the What-is-it truly was, although Father suspected it was a boy made up to look like a monkey. Still, it was exciting to behold, and Beth enjoyed it and the other freakish sights Mr. Barnum had collected.

Finally it came time for the Marches to return home. The train ride seemed as long going back to Concord as it had going to New York, but Beth and her parents had much to discuss. Father regaled them with stories told to him by Mr. Greeley, who, it seemed, knew everybody. The Marches were sharing their section with a German family who didn't speak any English, so Father felt free to tell his tales.

The longest part of the journey seemed to be from the train station in Concord to their home. Mr. Emerson met them, and he and Father had much to talk about, but Beth was so eager to see her sisters, she thought the ride would never end.

When they arrived home, Beth bounded out of the carriage. Jo was the first to greet her, and they exchanged hugs and kisses. Soon Beth had embraced Meg and Hannah as well. Amy, Beth noticed, hugged her parents but kept her distance from Beth. Beth was too overjoyed at being home to worry much about it.

It was too cold to stand outside, and the Marches rushed in to warm themselves by the fire. "I have presents for all of you," Beth told her sisters. "Let me open my bag and give them to you."

Meg seemed delighted by the piece of Irish

lace Beth had gotten for her, and Jo immediately sat down to read the volume of Washington Irving stories. But Amy merely glanced at the print of Central Park. Beth wondered what she should have brought instead.

"What did you get for yourself?" Meg asked.

"I didn't get anything," Beth replied.

"Not a single souvenir?" asked Jo.

"I didn't think to," said Beth.

"The picture of Father will be souvenir enough," said Marmee. "Meg, dear, there were no bargains to be found. New York is the most expensive city."

"And the most beautiful one," said Beth. "And the most exciting. And the biggest."

"Tell us everything," Jo demanded, and so Father, Marmee, and Beth spent the rest of the evening recounting all their New York experiences.

That night when Beth and Amy went to bed, they didn't talk as they usually did.

"How was your week?" Beth asked.

"It was fine," Amy replied. "Nothing happened."

"Surely something did," Beth said. She found it hard to believe that in a week when so much had happened to her, nothing had happened to Amy.

"I went to school," Amy said. "I did my chores. It was just as it always is. Now, if you don't mind, I'd like to go to sleep."

Beth did mind, but she didn't say anything. She told herself Amy would talk when she felt like it, but Amy kept to herself all weekend long.

By Monday, Beth was ready to return to school. New York already seemed very far away, and having missed a week of Miss Ramsey's class, Beth knew she'd have a great deal to catch up with. She and Amy took their seats at opposite ends of the room.

Miss Ramsey smiled at Beth. "Tell us about your trip," she said. "So few of us have ever been to New York."

Beth hated speaking in public. "There were a million people there. And a big park. Lots of theaters." She knew how inadequate that was. "We had a very nice time," she concluded, and sat down, hoping that would be the end of it.

And it would have been, except that Miss Ramsey said she had an announcement to make. "New York isn't the only place important people visit," she declared. "Tomorrow night, in Concord, Abraham Lincoln is coming to speak."

"I met him in New York," Beth said softly.

"Who's Abraham Lincoln?" Jesse Smith asked.

"He's running for president," Miss Ramsey replied. "He's hoping to get the Republican nomination. Beth, you saw him speak? I read about his talk in the newspaper."

"I didn't hear him speak," said Beth. "But I met him."

"Where would you meet somebody famous like that?" Jesse asked.

Beth wondered how it was that a minute before Jesse hadn't even heard of Mr. Lincoln and now he was too famous for Beth to have met. "I met him at Mr. Mathew Brady's studio," she said. "He sat on our bench and we talked."

"What did you talk about?" Mary Park asked.

"I told him women should be allowed to vote," Beth said.

"You did not," Gertrude Eberley said. "Beth March, you could hardly tell us what happened in New York, and now you expect us to believe you told someone who's running for president that women should be allowed to vote?"

Even Beth realized how funny that sounded. "He was very kind," she said. "And women *should* be allowed to vote."

"Miss Ramsey, Beth's making up stories," Charles Gordon said.

"I am not," Beth said. She wished Catherine Webster were there to back her up.

"Amy, did Beth tell you she met Abraham Lincoln?" Charles asked.

"Well, no," Amy said. "But you know Beth. She doesn't talk very much."

"I did meet Mr. Lincoln," Beth said, and she felt like crying. The one time she had spoken up in class, and nobody was willing to believe her—not her teacher or her classmates, and maybe not even Amy.

CHAPTER 7

" *I* didn't make it up," Beth told Meg, Jo, and Amy that night. The girls were preparing for bed when Beth told them the story. She had waited until then because she didn't want to worry her parents with her problems.

"Of course you didn't," Jo said. "You would never lie about anything, Beth."

"It was awful," Amy said. "Everybody felt that if Beth was lying, it meant I was a liar too."

"Did they say that to you?" Meg asked.

"No," Amy said. "But I was sure they felt it.

I really wish you hadn't spoken up, Beth. It made my day absolutely miserable."

"Oh, Amy," Jo said. "You weren't the one being tormented. It was poor Bethy."

"It's always 'poor Bethy,' " said Amy. "She gets the trips and she gets the pity." And Amy stormed out of Meg and Jo's room.

"I wish I had never gone to New York," Beth said. "I never would have if I'd known how upset it would make Amy."

"Amy's always upset about one thing or another," said Jo. "Leave her be and she'll come to her senses. My worry is what's to be done about you. Would you like me to go to your class tomorrow and tell them that I know you met Mr. Lincoln?"

"No," said Beth. "I never told you either."

"But that's just your nature," said Meg. "You always let others do the speaking, even at home. Marmee and Father had a thousand stories to tell, so naturally you didn't interrupt to tell us yours."

"And it really doesn't matter," Jo said.

"Just think, Beth. You met the man who might someday be president of the United States. What a story to tell your grandchildren."

"I only hope they'll believe me," Beth said, and she sounded so glum they all burst out laughing.

Beth and Amy hardly exchanged a word as they walked to school the next day. Matters weren't helped when Beth found a note saying "Liar" in her desk. She wiped away a tear, hoping no one had seen her, and determined that she would never say another word to anybody in the world ever again.

Classes went on as normal. Miss Ramsey rarely called on Beth anyway, since she knew of the girl's shyness. Beth tried to pay attention, but her thoughts strayed to New York, to Amy, and to Mr. Lincoln.

Right before lunchtime, there was a knock on the door. "Come in," said Miss Ramsey.

A very tall, very thin gentleman entered the

classroom. "I was told I might find a Miss Beth March in here," he said, looking around the sea of surprised faces.

"Mr. Lincoln!" Beth gasped.

"There you are," he said. "I remembered you'd said you lived in Concord, and I thought I'd drop by and say hello before I gave my talk this evening."

"W-Welcome to our classroom, M-Mr. Lincoln," Miss Ramsey stammered.

"Miss Beth and I had a nice chat at Mathew Brady's studio," Mr. Lincoln said. "It was the best thing that could have happened to me. I was rather nervous waiting for my portrait to be taken, and talking with Miss Beth relaxed me. The photograph is quite handsome as a result." He laughed. "If you can think of any picture of me being handsome, that is," he said.

A few of the children laughed. The rest seemed too startled to do anything except stare.

"I hope I'll have a chance to meet your family, Miss Beth," Mr. Lincoln said. "Your parents, and your sisters, Meg and Amy, as well as your brother, Joe."

At that, everyone in the class burst out laughing.

"What did I say that was so funny?" Mr. Lincoln asked.

"Jo's a girl," the class said in unison.

"He is?" Mr. Lincoln asked. "I mean, she is?"

"It's short for Josephine," Beth said, blushing. "I'm sorry. I just assumed you knew."

Mr. Lincoln chuckled. "The joke is on me," he said. "I was counting on his vote!"

The class laughed even harder.

"You see," Beth said, "that's why women should be allowed to vote."

"Perhaps you're right," Mr. Lincoln said. "I certainly intend to discuss it with my wife when I get back to Springfield."

"Springfield, Massachusetts?" one of Beth's classmates asked. "I have cousins who live there."

"I'm sure they're fine people," said Mr. Lincoln. "But I hail from Springfield, Illinois. I hope you won't hold that against me when it comes time for you to vote."

The class laughed some more.

"Here's a copy of my photograph," Mr. Lincoln said, walking over to Beth's desk. "What do you think?"

"It is a good picture," Beth said, examining it carefully. "But have you ever thought about growing a beard?"

"Can't say that I have," Mr. Lincoln said. "Do you think it would make me look more presidential?"

"Father has a beard," Beth said. "And he's quite the most dignified man. Isn't he, Amy?"

"Oh, is Amy in the class with you?" Mr. Lincoln asked. "Now, Amy is a girl, isn't she? I have that right, I trust."

Everyone except Amy laughed. Amy, Beth noticed, had turned bright red.

"This is my sister Amy," Beth said, gesturing toward her. "She's very much a girl. And she'd like to vote too."

"The Marches are an insistent group," said Mr. Lincoln. "At least I assume they are, based on Miss Beth here. Well, it's good to meet you, Miss Amy. I hope I'll see your whole family at the meeting tonight. All you children, tell your parents to come. There are a lot of important issues that have to be decided on in America, and the more informed its citizens are, the better we'll be able to deal with the crises at hand."

"Well put, Mr. Lincoln," said Miss Ramsey. "Thank you so much for visiting our class today."

"Thank you for allowing me to interrupt," he said. "Good-bye, Miss Beth. It was good to see you again." And as he left the room, Beth thought he was quite the nicest politician she'd ever met.

CHAPTER 8

"Just think, Beth," Gertrude said. "You know the man who might be president."

"And you spoke to him about women voting," Mary said.

"That was very brave of you, Beth," Miss Ramsey said. "We can all learn from you. We must tell our politicians what we believe in, so they can lead the country."

After school, everybody seemed excited that Beth March had met Abraham Lincoln. Everybody except Amy. She kept her distance while the other students flocked around Beth and demanded to hear every single word she had exchanged with Mr. Lincoln in New York and in Concord.

Even on the long walk home, Amy scarcely spoke. When Beth reached out to touch her, Amy broke away and ran the rest of the distance by herself.

When Beth got home, she told Marmee and Father about Mr. Lincoln's visit. Father had intended to hear him speak, and he readily agreed that the whole family should go.

"Someday my little women will have the vote," he said. "And the more they learn about politics, the better prepared they will be."

"I'm hoping someday I'll be able to vote as well," Marmee pointed out.

"I can think of few more qualified for that right," said Father. "And it's a grave injustice that you can't."

That night the meeting hall was filled mostly by men. Father was brought forward to be introduced to Mr. Lincoln. They talked a little longer than most of the other people Mr. Lincoln shook hands with. Beth hoped Mr. Lin-

coln had noticed how handsome Father looked with his beard.

Mr. Lincoln talked about slavery and abolition, but he failed to mention the need for women's suffrage. Still, Beth liked most of what he said and all of the way he said it. She especially liked his comment at the end of his speech. "Let us have faith that right makes might, and in that faith, let us, to the end, dare to do our duty as we understand it." Beth thought that was as true of women's rights as it was of freeing the slaves.

After he finished his talk, Mr. Lincoln was swamped by admirers. When Jo asked if they should push into the crowd so that Mr. Lincoln might have a chance to speak to Beth again, Father said no.

"Beth's had her moment with him," Father said. "Allow others that privilege."

If Jo was disappointed, she didn't act it. The Marches put on their hats and gloves and walked back to their home, talking of Mr. Lincoln, politics, and the possibility of war.

Beth and Amy undressed for bed as soon as they got home. Amy had continued her silence, and Beth decided she had had enough.

"You can't keep quiet forever," she told her younger sister in their dark, cold bedroom.

"I don't intend to forever," Amy said. "I'll talk when I'm ready to."

"And when will that be?" Beth demanded.

"When the real Beth comes back," Amy said.

"Who do you think I am?" Beth asked.

"Some imposter," Amy said.

Beth could hardly see her sister, the room was so dark. "Are you joking?" she asked. "I'm Beth March, and you know it."

"The Beth March I know isn't selfish," Amy said. "And she doesn't draw attention to herself."

"How did I draw attention to myself?" Beth asked. She didn't care for Amy's tone, but it was more than her younger sister had said to her since before the trip, and Beth supposed it was better than nothing.

"'I know Mr. Lincoln,'" Amy said in a mocking tone. "'We're the best of friends. I told him just how he should run the country. And my big brother Joe agrees with me one hundred percent.'"

"I never said any of those things," Beth said. "And I only mentioned meeting Mr. Lincoln because his name came up."

"I wish you had kept quiet," Amy said. "It makes me look bad when you look bad."

"And looking good is more important than loving me?" Beth asked. "Or don't you love me at all?"

Beth thought she'd never heard anything so awful as Amy's silence. It seemed like forever before Amy spoke. "Of course I love you," she finally said. "Everyone loves you. I just wish they loved me as much as they loved you."

"Who loves me more than they love you?" Beth asked.

"Jo, for one," said Amy. "She always sides with you."

Beth wanted to say that Jo loved Amy every

bit as much, but she suspected that wasn't true. She and Jo had a special relationship, and Amy was certain to have noticed it.

"You and Jo fight all the time," Beth said instead. "If you didn't fight so much, you'd know how much Jo loves you."

"Sometimes I think Marmee loves you more too," said Amy. "And Father. You're so good, Beth, and they think being good is so important."

"It is important," Beth said.

"But it comes so easily to you," Amy said. "If I'd gone to New York, I wouldn't have brought home presents for anybody but myself. I would have spent all my money on me."

"No, you wouldn't have," Beth said, shaking her head. "You're not selfish, Amy."

"I am too," Amy said, and she began to cry. "I hated you for going to New York when I wanted to so much."

"I'm sorry I went," Beth said. "I wish it had been you and not me."

"Stop it!" Amy shouted. "That's just the

kind of thing I mean. You should be glad you got to go. I would have been. I wouldn't have felt bad for my sisters being stuck in miserable old Concord. I would have enjoyed every moment with hardly a second thought about them."

It was Beth's turn to be silent a moment. "You know, that is how I felt," she said at last. "When I left, I thought my heart would break being away from you all for a whole week. And I suppose there were moments during that week that I did miss you. But mostly I had such a wonderful time, I didn't think of you nearly as often as I thought I would. I just had a good time. I never realized how selfish I am. I'm a terrible person."

Amy giggled.

"What are you laughing at?" Beth asked.

"You," Amy said. "And how terrible you are."

"It's nothing to laugh about," Beth said.

"I suppose not," Amy said. "Are you going to tell Mr. Lincoln the next time you see him?"

"Do you think I should?" Beth asked.

"No, don't," Amy said. "He might decide women shouldn't vote after all!" And she burst into such loud laughter that Meg and Jo ran into the room.

"What's going on in here?" Meg asked. "Don't you know little girls should be asleep by now?"

"Not if they're as bad as we are," Beth said, and she and Amy laughed all the harder at the shocked silence that greeted that remark.

"Little sisters," Jo said to Meg. "How do we ever endure them?"

"And how could we ever endure without them?" asked Meg.

"I hope we never have to," Beth said, giving her own little sister a great big hug.

PORTRAITS OF LITTLE WOMEN ACTIVITIES

OLD-FASHIONED GINGERSNAPS

These cookies, spiced with ginger and sweetened with molasses, are as popular and delicious today as they were in Louisa May Alcott's time.

INGREDIENTS

    3/4 cup melted and cooled butter or margarine

    1 cup granulated sugar, plus more for rolling cookies

    1/4 cup molasses

    1 egg

    2 cups flour

    2 teaspoons baking soda

    1/2 teaspoon ground cloves

    1/2 teaspoon ground ginger

    1 teaspoon ground cinnamon

    1/2 teaspoon salt

Preheat oven to 375 degrees.

1. Combine butter, sugar, molasses, and egg and beat until creamy.
2. Sift flour, baking soda, spices, and salt into butter mixture. Combine well.
3. Sprinkle additional granulated sugar onto a piece of wax paper.
4. Form dough into 1-inch balls and roll them in sugar.
5. Place dough balls 2 inches apart on lightly greased cookie sheets.
6. Bake in preheated oven about 10 minutes. Tops will begin to crackle.
7. Remove from sheets immediately and let cool.

Makes about 5 dozen cookies.

Serve with your favorite iced tea, lemonade, or a glass of milk.

DRIED FLOWER BOUQUET

There is something very romantic about a bouquet of dried flowers. Whether in a vase, hung on a wall, or laid atop a table, they add beauty and a touch of elegance.

FLOWERS
Baby's breath
Daisies
Flax
Hydrangeas
Lavender
Mini-carnations
Pansies
Roses
Statice
Violets
Any small flowers

OTHER MATERIALS

Florist's wire, twist-ties, or rubber bands
Scissors
Velvet, satin, or silk ribbons

1. Choose among flowers listed above. You can buy them at your local flower shop or cut them from your own garden.
2. Tie together in bunches with florist's wire, twist-ties, or rubber bands.
3. Hang flowers upside down (from a door-knob, hook, or clothesline) using florist's wire.
4. Allow flowers to dry. This takes one to two weeks.
5. Arrange dried flowers in a bouquet of any size. Experiment with flower combinations or use only one kind of flower.
6. Cut stems to desired length.
7. Tie a pretty ribbon(s) around stems.

Place bouquet in a favorite vase or on your dresser, or hang from your curtains or wall.

A dried flower bouquet makes a very nice present for a special friend.

Read all about Louisa May Alcott's
unforgettable heroines in
Portraits of Little Women:

Meg's Story

Jo's Story

Beth's Story

Amy's Story

Here are sample chapters from each of the
other three delightful stories.

Meg's Story

CHAPTER 1

eg March looked at her slate and sighed. Would the school day never end?

Ordinarily Meg enjoyed school. She loved to read, and she liked history as well. Her family was a part of American history. Two of her great-grandfathers had fought in the American Revolution. Even arithmetic, which was what her class was supposed to be working on just then, could be interesting.

But not on the first day of June. Not when the sun was shining and the classroom, which had been cold all winter long, was warm enough to encourage dozing. Not when she and her sisters were halfway through their most recent play, which would, of course, star Meg and Jo. Beth had agreed to play the piano for the play, and Amy was now old enough to memorize lines and could be given small parts to perform. It was certain to be their best production ever.

And the day was so lovely that when they got home, they could work on the play in the garden. So why wouldn't the school day end?

Meg looked quickly toward Jo's seat. Jo was a year younger, and they were in the same classroom. Beth and Amy were in a classroom for younger children. Meg wondered if they were as impatient as she was for lessons to be over. Jo was, she knew, but Jo was impatient about everything.

Meg feared she might explode, but fortunately the bell rang and the teacher dismissed the class. Meg noticed that he too seemed relieved, and she supposed it couldn't be fun to rein in the spirits of twenty-five children aged nine through eleven on a beautiful afternoon in June. Her parents frequently told her to be considerate of the feelings of others. Meg was pleased with herself that she cared about her teacher's feelings. She doubted Jo thought of him at all.

In fact, Jo had already escaped from the school by the time Meg reached the front door. Meg waited a moment, until Beth and Amy appeared, and then they walked out together. Jo, she noted, was racing with some of the boys from their class. Jo was the best runner in their class, and she never minded letting the boys know that.

"Jo isn't very ladylike," Amy said as they watched their sister win yet another race.

"Jo isn't ladylike at all," replied Meg.

"But you're a lady, Meg," said Beth.

"I'm more of one than Jo, but not nearly as much of one as Amy," Meg replied with a laugh.

"You can laugh," Amy said, "but I intend to marry great wealth someday, and I'll be more of a lady than anybody else in this town has ever been."

"Concord has many ladies," Beth said. "Doesn't it, Meg? Aunt March is a lady. And Marmee is the best lady of all."

"Amy means the kind of lady who wears silks and laces all the time," Meg said. "And doesn't make do with mended calicoes."

"You have no right to complain," said Amy. "I have it worst of all. Practically every dress I've ever owned you wore once, then Jo and then Beth. It wouldn't be so bad if it were just you, or even you and Beth. But Jo rips everything, and I spend half my life in patches." She looked so mournful that Meg burst out laughing again.

"Meg March! Wait for me!"

Meg turned around and saw Mary Howe calling for her. Mary was in the same class as Meg and Jo. And she was definitely Amy's idea of a lady. It was clear that Mary had never worn a patched piece of clothing in her life.

"Meg, I want to speak to you," Mary said as she joined the March sisters.

"Certainly, Mary," said Meg. Beth, always shy, was hiding as best she could behind Meg. Amy was staring straight at Mary, drinking in the details of Mary's perfect blue dress and its white lace collar.

"I'm having a picnic on Saturday," Mary announced. "My brother, Willie, and I. Mama said I could invite three girls and Willie could invite three boys. Willie's asked Freddie and James and George. I've asked Priscilla Browne and Sallie Gardiner and now I'm asking you. Do say you'll come. Sallie Gardiner has often said it's not your fault your family has so little money, and I agree. You're quite the nicest girl in our class, and very ladylike in spite of your family's straits."

"Why, thank you," Meg said. "A picnic sounds lovely."

"It will be," said Mary. "We'll play games and eat ice cream and have the most wonderful time."

"I'll have to ask my mother first," Meg said. "But if she says I may, I'd love to attend your picnic."

"I'm so glad," Mary said. "Please tell your mother that my mother thinks she is the most splendid lady. Tell me tomorrow whether you can come. The picnic will be at one o'clock on Saturday. I do hope you'll attend." She took Meg's hand and gave it an affectionate squeeze, then walked away to join her brother, Willie.

Meg was so delighted, she laughed out loud with joy.

Jo's Story

CHAPTER 1

"*J*osephine! Josephine March!"

Jo March sighed and turned to face Aunt March. Only Aunt March called her Josephine, and only Aunt March used that tone of voice with her.

"Yes, Aunt March?" she asked.

"What is that book in your hand?" Aunt March demanded.

"It's *Oliver Twist*, Aunt," Jo replied. "By Charles Dickens."

"I know who wrote *Oliver Twist*, young lady," said Aunt March. "That book came off my shelves, did it not?"

"Yes, Aunt March," Jo said. Aunt March's library was the best thing about visiting her great-aunt. Actually, Aunt March's library was the *only* thing Jo enjoyed about visiting her great-aunt. But visit she must, or so her parents said.

"*Oliver Twist* is not suitable reading matter for a child," proclaimed Aunt March. "Put it back on the shelves."

"But Father reads Dickens to us all the time," Jo said. "He's read us *David Copperfield* and *Little Dorrit* and *A Christmas Carol*. *The Pickwick Papers* is my favorite book of all. But I've never read *Oliver Twist,* and I've always wanted to. Please let me borrow it."

"Perhaps your father agrees with me that *Oliver Twist* is unsuitable for such a young girl," said Aunt March.

"I'm not so young," Jo said. "I'm ten already."

"And a rude young girl, at that," Aunt March declared. "I sometimes wonder what kind of manners your parents are teaching you."

"Father and Marmee are the best parents in the world," said Jo angrily. "Don't you speak against them."

"And don't you use that tone with me, young lady," Aunt March said. "Have your parents never taught you to respect your elders?"

"Of course they have," Jo said.

"Then the fault must lie with you and not them," said Aunt March, "for I'm sure you're showing me no respect at all."

Jo could have kicked herself. All she wanted was to get this visit over with as fast as she possibly could. That meant not quarreling with Aunt March. Jo had simply become so excited when she'd found the copy of *Oliver Twist*, she'd forgotten her mission of getting in and out in a half hour's time.

"I'm sorry, Aunt March," said Jo, and she was sorry—sorry she'd aroused Aunt March's wrath, since it meant she'd be there for at least another ten minutes and would probably go home without the precious Dickens volume to read.

"I will never understand why you can't be more like your sister Margaret," said Aunt March. "Now, there's a girl your parents can be proud of. She's every inch a lady."

"Yes, Aunt March," Jo said. She tried to hide the copy of *Oliver Twist* in the folds of her skirt. "Meg is a lady."

"You could learn something from your sister Beth as well," said Aunt March. "Quiet as a church mouse and never causing any trouble."

"Yes, Aunt March," Jo said.

"Even little Amy could teach you a thing or two," said Aunt March. "She is such a darling child, so pretty and artistic. Not at all the sort of child who talks back."

"Yes, Aunt March," Jo said for what felt like the hundredth time. Of course Aunt

March had a point. Meg was a lady—always polite, always willing to help others. Beth was a dear, sweet and kind—everyone loved her. Amy was pretty and artistic, and even if she drove Jo to distraction, she was the sort of child Aunt March would favor.

And Jo was just the sort of girl that Aunt March would want to improve. Jo was sharp-tongued, quick-tempered, and boyish.

"I suppose your parents have done as good a job as they could raising you girls, having so little money and so many ideals," Aunt March declared. "Your sisters, at least, are a credit to them."

"I'll try to be better," said Jo. "I want to be a credit to Marmee and Father."

Aunt March shook her head. "I've heard you make that promise a hundred times before, Josephine," she said, "but I've rarely seen you live up to it."

"It's hard," Jo blurted out. "I'm not Meg and I'm not Beth and I'm not Amy. Goodness comes so easily to them. To Meg and Beth, at least. And people always forgive Amy her mistakes because of her blond curls and pretty ways."

"You might not have Amy's blond curls," said Aunt March, "but couldn't you learn from her pretty ways?"

Jo thought about it for a moment. "No," she said, "I don't think I could."

Aunt March stared at Jo, and then, much to Jo's surprise, she laughed out loud. "I suspect you're right," she said. "Very well. You've paid your old aunt her visit. You may go home now."

"Thank you, Aunt March," Jo said. She walked over to her aunt and gave her a kiss on the cheek.

"But give me back *Oliver Twist*," said Aunt March. "When I speak to your parents next, I'll ask them if they approve of it for you. If the answer is yes, you may borrow it the next time you visit me."

"Oh, thank you, Aunt," said Jo, knowing

that was far better than she could have hoped for. And the visit was over. It was all she could do to keep from skipping out of her great-aunt's house as she escaped and turned toward home.

Amy's Story

CHAPTER 1

"What do you want most in the world, Amy?" Jo March asked her youngest sister.

It was a Saturday afternoon in April. There was a scent of springtime in the air, but it was too cold for Amy and her sisters, Meg, Jo, and Beth, to be playing outside. Instead they were in the parlor. Their parents were visiting their friends the Emersons.

Amy could recall a time when she and her sisters were regarded as too young to be left alone. But now Meg was fifteen, Jo fourteen, Beth twelve, and Amy almost eleven.

"Why do you want to know?" Amy asked.

"I was just wondering," Jo replied. "I know what I want the most: to be a famous writer. And Meg wants a husband and babies. Am I right, Meg?"

"I would like a husband and babies," Meg said with a smile. "But not for another week or two, thank you. Right now what I'd like more than anything is a new dress. One I could wear to parties and not be ashamed of."

"You have nothing to be ashamed of," Beth said. "You dress beautifully, Meg."

Meg sighed. "Not compared to the girls I know. Anyway, that's what I want. A pretty new party dress."

"I want all of us to be happy," said Beth. "And some new sheet music. And a really fine piano. And a new head for my doll. Her headless body looks so sad."

"That's quite a list," Jo said. "Now, Amy, what's your pleasure?"

"A truly aristocratic nose," Amy replied.

"You ought to know, Jo, since it's your fault I don't have one."

"Will you never let me forget?" Jo said. "I didn't mean to drop you when you were a baby. I suppose you must have been quite slippery."

"You couldn't be any prettier than you are now," Beth told Amy. "And I think your nose is extremely aristocratic. For an American, that is."

"Beth's right," said Jo. "A true patriot wouldn't care so much for an aristocratic nose, Amy. You are a true patriot, aren't you?"

"As much a one as you," Amy said. "But there's nothing in the Constitution that prevents me from wanting a truly beautiful nose."

"You're beautiful enough as you are," said Meg. "What else would you like?"

Amy thought about it. She knew she was pretty. Her shiny blond hair fell in lovely curls, and her eyes were as blue as cornflowers. Still, an aristocratic nose would help, but beyond sleeping with a clothespin on her nose there was little she could do to make it perfect.

"I'd like to be a real, professional artist," she said. "Someone who sells her paintings for lots and lots of money."

"I'd like that too," Jo said. "For you're a generous girl, Amy, and sure to share your wealth with your less fortunate sisters!"

The girls laughed. They were still laughing when their parents entered the parlor.

"What a wonderful greeting," Father said. "My little women enjoying themselves so."

"Father, Marmee!" the girls cried, and although they had seen their parents just a few hours earlier, they rushed into their arms and exchanged embraces.

"It is good to see you so happy," Marmee said. "Especially after the conversation we just had with the Emersons."

"Why, Marmee?" Beth asked. "Everything's all right with them, isn't it?"

"With them, yes," Father replied. "But not with the nation."

"You mean the Southern states seceding?" Jo asked. "President Lincoln will keep the country together. I'm sure of it."

"It will take more than words," said Father. "It was in the newspapers. The Confederates have fired upon Fort Sumter."

"Where's that, Father?" asked Meg. Amy was glad Meg had asked, as she didn't care to appear ignorant.

"It's in Charleston, South Carolina. The Union soldiers were asked to surrender but refused, and the Southerners fired upon them."

"How terrible," Meg said. "Were there fatalities?"

"Fortunately not," said Father. "But we'd be naive to think there won't be. War has begun, and with war there is always loss and suffering."

"I wish I were a boy," said Jo. "I'd enlist right away to fight for the Union and for the end of slavery."

"I'm glad I have daughters and no sons," said Marmee. "I know it's selfish of me, but at least I don't have to worry about any of you dying in battle. No matter how noble the cause."

"You aren't going to go off to be a soldier, are you, Father?" asked Beth.

"I'm too old, I'm afraid," Father said. "But there must be something I can do. All these years, I've fought for abolition. But what are words when young men are going to sacrifice their lives?"

"Words are what you have to offer," said Marmee. "And prayers too, for a quick resolution to this war."

War. Amy thrilled at the very word. She had no desire to be a boy and go off to fight. But, like Jo, she found the idea of war exciting. Handsome young men in uniform, fighting for a just and noble cause.

She supposed some of the men fighting for the South were handsome as well, but she didn't care. They were certain to lose and to realize how wrong they were about everything.

"It's a good war, isn't it, Father?" she asked.

Father sighed. "All wars are evil. But in this case, there's a greater evil, and that's slavery. So in some ways, it's a good war. But I pray it will be a short one, with as little bloodshed as possible."

"That's what we all should pray for," Marmee said.

Amy thought about her nose. It was selfish of her to wish for a nicer one when young men were going to risk their lives for the freedom of others.

"I'll pray for a short war, Father," Amy said. "And for freedom for the slaves."

Her father smiled at her. "I know you will, Amy. And I know my daughters will do everything they can to help the cause. Sacrifices will have to be made. There are always sacrifices in times of war. But you'll do what you have to to alleviate the suffering of others."

"We will, I promise," said Meg. "We'll do whatever we can for the Union and for abolition."

Amy wondered what she would have to sacrifice. Anything but the clothespin, she thought, then realized she was still being selfish. Anything at all, she promised. She would sacrifice anything at all for the Union and abolition.

ABOUT THE AUTHOR OF
PORTRAITS OF LITTLE WOMEN

SUSAN BETH PFEFFER is the author of both middle-grade and young adult fiction. Her middle-grade novels include *Nobody's Daughter* and its companion, *Justice for Emily*. Her highly praised *The Year Without Michael* is an ALA Best Book for Young Adults, an ALA YALSA Best of the Best, and a *Publishers Weekly* Best Book of the Year. Her novels for young adults include *Twice Taken, Most Precious Blood, About David*, and *Family of Strangers*. Susan Beth Pfeffer lives in Middletown, New York.

A WORD ABOUT
LOUISA MAY ALCOTT

LOUISA MAY ALCOTT was born in 1832 in
Germantown, Pennsylvania, and grew up in
the Boston-Concord area of Massachusetts.
She received her early education from her father, Bronson Alcott, a renowned educator
and writer, who eventually left teaching to
study philosophy. To supplement the family
income, Louisa worked as a teacher, a house-
hold servant, and a seamstress, and she wrote
stories as well as poems for newspapers and
magazines. In 1868 she published the first volume of *Little Women*, a novel about four sisters
growing up in a small New England town during the Civil War. The immediate success of
Little Women made Louisa May Alcott a cele-
brated writer, and the novel remains one of
today's best-loved books. Alcott wrote until
her death in 1888.